Elle & Buddy

written by
K. D. Rausin

illustrated by
Muza Ulasowski

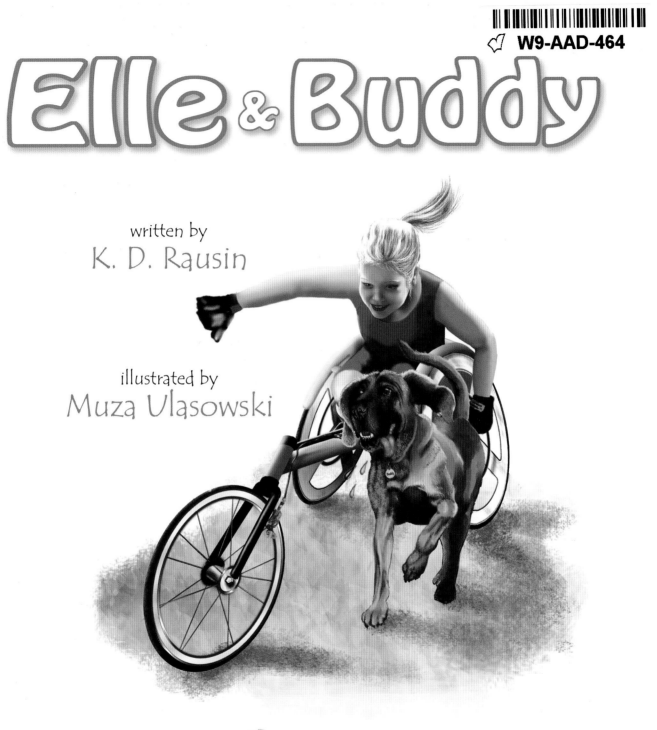

Peter E. Randall
PUBLISHER
www.PERpublisher.com

Elle peeked through her fingers and counted the cars on the Ferris wheel.

"Oh no, I'm not going up there! It's too high!"

The cars at the tippy-top dropped down from the clouds like summer rain.

3

"Don't worry, Buddy. We're staying down here."

Slobber dripped from his jowls. Eeeeeew!

Elle swiped it away, then wheeled to the car.

On the way home a flash of red caught Elle's eye.
A boy was racing around a track.

"WOW!" shouted Elle.

"That's a racing wheelchair," said Mama.
"Let's watch."

Buddy popped his head out the window.
Slobber flew through the air.

Eeeeew!

Elle laughed.
"See how fast he's flying!"

Three racing wheelchairs whooshed by—a shiny red one, a turquoise one and a bright yellow one with a green stripe.

Punch - glide
Punch - glide

The racers
hit the wheels
with their gloved hands.

11

Elle cheered for her favorite.

Yay!!

The boy in the red racing
wheelchair crossed
the finish line
first.

That night Elle spent hours
sketching a special picture.

She taped it
to her wall and
made a wish...

"If I had a racing
wheelchair, I'd be
the fastest girl in
the world!"

CRAYONS

Elle decorated her room like a track. Buddy collapsed across lanes one and two.

She dreamed of
flying across the
finish line with
hundreds of
people clapping
and chanting:

FINISH
61

"Elle! Elle!"

Buddy would be adorned with her medals and he'd wave his giant paw at the crowd.

Then one morning Elle
woke to a fantastic surprise...
a racing wheelchair!

"Yippee!"

Buddy presented her with a helmet.
Slobber slid down the strap.

Elle giggled.

Every day Elle practiced racing.

Buddy galloped alongside.

23

Elle sailed through the park past palm trees. Geckos scurried out of her way as she soared down sidewalks.

Faster and faster she rode until Buddy could no longer keep up. Wind whooshed across her face.

KEEP OFF GRASS

Mama insisted they break for sips of water.
Elle harrumphed.
Buddy lapped up three gallons!

Buddy wanted to race too!

Elle gave him a squeeze.

"You'll always be my best Buddy!"

The next year when Elle spotted the giant Ferris wheel, she shouted: "C'mon, Buddy, let's go! Now that I can fly in my racing wheelchair, a silly Ferris wheel doesn't scare me. I'll race you to the tippy-top!"

FERRIS
WHEEL
TICKETS

The real Elle:

Arielle Rausin was born on September 16, 1993 in Santa Monica, California. At the age of ten she was paralyzed in a car accident. When Arielle was in seventh grade, her P. E. teacher, Ms. Black, challenged her to run a 5K and join her middle school track team. Arielle ran her first few races in her everyday wheelchair and then discovered racing wheelchairs. Florida history was made...

In 2009, when Arielle wanted to join her high school track team, she was told she was not allowed. The Florida High School Athletic Association did not recognize adaptive sports. Arielle advocated for herself and with the help of the community, Loretta Purish, Scot Hollonbeck and Lew Friedland, the FHSAA developed an adaptive track program in 2010 for high school athletes across Florida.

Today, Arielle Rausin is an athlete on the University of Illinois wheelchair racing team.

K. D. Rausin:

K. D. Rausin lives in sunny Florida with a house full of animals, her husband and two kids. ELLE & BUDDY is her second children's book.
Her website:
www.KDRausin.com

Muza Ulasowski:

Muza Ulasowski lives in sunny Brisbane, Australia with her husband, a vast array of local wildlife and their bulldog. She has illustrated 9 picture books to date.
Her website:
www.muzadesigns.com.au

Works Consulted

1. 2014 Boston Marathon, Media Guide:
   http://www.bostonmarathonmediaguide.com/9-synopsis.php

2. Florida High School Athletic Association, Adapted Track and Field:
   http://www.fhsaa.org/sports/track-field-adapted

3. Mandeville Legacy, Wheelchair Racing:
   http://www.mandevillelegacy.org.uk/page.aspx?id=99

4. The Museum of Modern Art, The Collection:
   http://www.moma.org/collection//browse_results.php?
   criteria=O%3AAD%3AE%3A2462&page_number=1&template
   _id=1&sort_order=1&background=gray

5. Paralympics, History of the Movement:
   http://www.paralympic.org/the-ipc/history-of-the-movement

can you find all the geckos?

Kids:

If you know anyone who is interested in adaptive sports,
have them check out the Challenged Athletes Foundation!

http://www.challengedathletes.org